T0001234

POEMS ABOUT BIRDS

More nature writing available from
Macmillan Collector's Library

The Gardener's Year by Karel Capek

Our Place in Nature edited by Zachary Seager

The Joy of Walking edited by Suzy Cripps

Green Shades edited by Elizabeth Jane Howard

Poems of the Sea introduced by Adam Nicolson

Poems on Nature introduced by Helen Macdonald

POEMS ABOUT BIRDS

Edited and introduced by
H. J. MASSINGHAM

MACMILLAN COLLECTOR'S LIBRARY

First published 1922

This edition first published 2023 by Macmillan Collector's Library
an imprint of Pan Macmillan
The Smithson, 6 Briset Street, London EC1M 5NR
EU representative: Macmillan Publishers Ireland Ltd, 1st Floor,
The Liffey Trust Centre, 117–126 Sheriff Street Upper,
Dublin 1, DO1 YC43
Associated companies throughout the world
www.panmacmillan.com

ISBN 978-1-5290-9626-2

1 3 5 7 9 8 6 4 2

A CIP catalogue record for this book is available from the British Library.

Cover and endpaper design: Katie Tooke, Pan Macmillan Art Department
Typeset in Plantin by Jouve (UK), Milton Keynes
Printed and bound in China by Imago

Visit **www.panmacmillan.com** to read more
about all our books and to buy them.

Contents

FROM THE NINETEENTH TO THE TWENTIETH CENTURY

TWENTIETH CENTURY

Introduction

H. J. MASSINGHAM

Some words are necessary to explain the scope and method of this collection. I do not profess to be one of those compilers who apologise for their wares on the grounds that there are too many of them. Why add another, then, is the answer for a gift. Neither do I share the minority prejudice against anthologies as such. They may be good or bad, useful or worthless, but to condemn them for being what they are seems to me a form of literary snobbery. Apart from the question of relative merit—and to make a really good anthology is a much harder job than the writing of many "original" works—I can see only one serious objection to them. They may influence their readers against going to the originals from which the selections are taken and so encourage a light-minded and surface culture. But the blame is surely the readers', for the proper anthology should open rather than shut the door to the strongroom of the bank of literature by exhibiting some handfuls of its best money. Granted all the shoddy, a competent anthology seems to me of real value in inspiring and diffusing a taste for and knowledge of literature, which education lacks and needs more than anything else.

The object of this one is also to foster what I believe is a native and growing appreciation of natural life and beauty, which will in time rout the huge vested interests in destruction of life for frivolous purposes, from the egger to the milliner. Not the least of my difficulties has been to keep the balance between the two demands. But as bad poetry means bad thinking, and bad thinking bad feeling, I have given priority to the first and omitted the incredible amount of inferior verse which takes birds as its subject matter. My publisher never suggested a wiser thing than that I should keep the book within the limits of two hundred poems, and I do not believe that beyond its frontier there exist more than a very few tolerable ones in the whole language. If so, I have missed them. I do not of course pretend that all of these collected here are of first-class quality, but I do claim that they take poetic honours of some kind, so far as I am a judge of them.

I have also tried to keep an eye to their being as representative as possible of the several ages in which they were written, and so of the different stages the poetic mind has passed in its emotional response to nature. The reasons for my chronological arrangement of the text I propose to give later, as they embrace an interesting problem. The poems are grouped into four divisions, the first containing those written between the Middle Ages and the Restoration; the second during the eighteenth century; the third (beginning with Blake) representing dead writers beyond it; and the fourth those written in the twentieth century.

Poetry is essentially ideal. Imitation of nature as an end and for its own sake is the death of all art. The first and last law of poetry, an element which absorbs and transforms every other element upon which it works into something new, is to be true to itself.

It is an axiom that evolution works by a slow integration of all things, not in spite of but through their distinctness and particularity, and this maxim can, I think, be applied to the relations of poetry to nature and is the reason for the chronological arrangement of this book. Man's perception of beauty in nature is vastly older than his discovery of metals, older than his very speech, and the first articulate word from his lispings was beauty. Coleridge neither saw the landscape of the "Ancient Mariner" nor got it out of a book, for Shelvocke's "Voyages" is a sunless sea indeed. It was etched upon his mind by intuitive memory, mysteriously quickened in all true poetic natures, just as the essential form of the charging mammoth sprang from the dripping walls of the sepulchral limestone grotto at the will of a hand with no living model before it. How richly revealing, indeed, of man's foster-childhood to nature for tens of thousands of years are those polychromatic mural frescoes of the unstoried Cro-Magnon race! The sense of beauty, of that nth power in nature all her great artists glorify, is an inheritance so fundamental to us that it is in the marrow of our bones and the pigment of our blood. Who knows what Coleridge (to go still farther back) did not owe to the lemurine anthropoid creeping among the tree-tops and receiving through the cracks of his shut mind the light capering among the leaves? Nature's beauty is an instinctive patrimony to man born of nature; and to acknowledge that gift in a thousand different ways and through a hundred different materials revealing the Creator in the creature, is the function of art. A deepening and expanding sense of beauty, the climbing of a hill only to see a mountain beyond it, is part of our evolution, the most important part, and every artist who creates beauty is going back to nature, whether he knows it or not.

"Nature-poetry" is the explicit recognition of this legacy. There are colours in the spectrum imperceptible to the human eye, but visible to the super-eye. The mission of the artist is to see things that do not meet the eye, and his perceptions are intuitive. We have in fact to look at nature-poetry in two ways: as a work of art, a thing in itself, and relatively to the age and status of discovery in which it was written. What was right for the Elizabethans is wrong for us, because our modern life has won new attitudes to and knowledge from nature to them unknown except in uncertain gleams. It is not that we find disharmonies among the Elizabethans and still earlier poets, and that their expression of values is wrong because it is different from ours. In the seventeenth century, the mind often robs the senses; in the Renaissance proper, fancy takes conventional liberties with matter and experience, and arranges them in formal patterns. Nature was a kind of Clarkson to the Elizabethans, and a limited type of costume was *de rigueur*. We should be wrong to find fault with them on that account, since the convention was well and truly adapted to the needs and resources of the period, and in its own place evokes the full chords of beauty. The nature-poetry of the Middle Ages, again, partly shows us the later method in the making (in the convention of May-Day, for instance), and partly something set apart and peculiar to their own special and more concrete genius. Nature is delightfully humanised, as religion was, and beasts and birds and saints and angels and devils play a united part in the theatre of human destiny. The eighteenth-century pastoralists, again, break fresh ground; their method, or rather system, is what science calls a "mutation" towards the objective and descriptive treatment of nature, and in the hands of Thomson and Cowper the new instrument yielded its full volume of sound. But Thomson, the centre of the new movement, is at the same time its worst enemy. Poetry is always breaking into and out of his set numbers, just as the robins hop in and out of the glass house at Kew and thrill the academy of alien growths with their native warble.

With the nineteenth century, launched by Blake and Burns, that intuitive memory, implanted by nature, seemed to become self-conscious and aware of its source, and the spiral of evolution took a new turn. Its first glory has as good a name in the Realistic as in the Romantic Revival, for a leap forward in poetic power and range of vision corresponded with a more intimate perception of natural truth. Roughly, the age began to see things in and for themselves, to realise an immortal aspect of beauty behind them, and to gain a new reverence for life as it acquired a truer knowledge of it. Poetry became both more particular and more integral, and it was natural that this modern turn, with its more and more sympathetic understanding of the nature of things, should be shot through with portents of Darwinism, which demonstrates the growth of integration and differentiation in the natural world. The bond between nature and the soul of man was recognised, and Coleridge defines beauty in the abstract as "the unity of the manifold, the coalescence of the diverse." The age of unity in nature-poetry had dawned, and it sought balances and reconciliations in every direction, with "truth to nature," with "humanitarianism," with knowledge, and with the spirit of nature urging its manifold forms into life.

"Truth to nature," therefore, has become very wide in meaning. Professor Thomson says of the nature-poets that they are "the truest because deepest biologists of us all"—that is one truth, to penetrate matter and read the Sibyl's mysteries. Another, surely, is some knowledge by sense or intuition of the external processes of nature, as a key to nature's language, a passage between it and the soul of man, a treasure-house of imagery and illustration and a parable of effortless expression. Many artists fight shy of this knowledge as impeding their freedom. But the genuine artist turns all to good, and to make bread grinds all that he can gather into his mill. New knowledge is new words, new colours, new thoughts, new beauties to him.

It can be fairly claimed that this little world of poems about birds is a globe reflecting these larger movements and currents more graciously and compactly than a more ambitious volume could accomplish. Birds enter into nature like stars into the sky, quickening her pulse and revealing the graces of her spirit. Without them her blood runs too cold for sun or central fires to warm it. They were a sudden, bright thought of hers, run into rhyme, and ever after have been the expression of her lyrical power, easing with laughter and at the same time articulating after long travail those mighty impulses of life, love, death, and birth whose purposes she broods. How naturally, then, do these living songs lend wings and voices to the poets, reaching up to where:

> "The gods embrace
> And stars are born and suns: . . .
> . . . where life and death are one"—

and catching in the curves, eddies, circles, sweeps of music and flight the tumults of the human heart.

"Come tell us, O tell us,
    Thou strange mortality!
What's *thy* thought of us, Dear?—
    Here's *our* thought of thee."
                FRANCIS THOMPSON.

"Music . . . an art common to men and birds."
                ANATOLE FRANCE.

"True to the kindred points of Heaven
            and Home."
                WORDSWORTH.

FROM THE MIDDLE AGES TO
THE RESTORATION

Sparrows and Men

I

Man's life is like a Sparrow, mighty King!
That, stealing in, while by the fire you sit
Housed with rejoicing friends, is seen to flit
Safe from the storm, in comfort tarrying.
Here did it enter—there, on hasty wing
Flies out, and passes on from cold to cold;
But whence it came we know not, nor behold
Whither it goes. E'en such that transient Thing,
The human Soul; not utterly unknown
While in the Body lodged, her warm abode:—
But from what world She came, what woe or
   weal
On her departure waits, no tongue hath shewn:
This mystery if the Stranger can reveal,
His be a welcome cordially bestowed!

The Venerable Bede (673–735)

The Cage

Tak any brid, and put it in a cage,
And do al thyn entente, and thy corage
To fostre it tendrely with mete and drinke,
Of alle deyntees that thou canst bithinke,
And kepe it al so clenly as thou may;
Al-though his cage of gold be never so gay,
Yet hath this brid, by twenty thousand fold,
Lever in a forest, that is rude and cold,
Gon ete wormes and swich wretchednesse.
For ever this brid wol doon his bisinesse
To escape out of his cage, if he may:
His liberty this brid desireth ay.

Geoffrey Chaucer (1340–1400)

A May Burden

And on the smalle greenè twistis sat
The little sweetè nightingale, and sung
So loud and clear the hymnès consecrat
Of lovè's use: now soft, now loud among,
That all the gardens and the wallès rung
  Right of their song . . .

Worship, ye that lovers been, this May,
For of your bliss the Kalends are begun;
And sing with us, "Away, winter, away!
Come, summer, come, the sweet season and
  sun!
Awake, for shame, that have your heavens
  won,
And amorously lift up your headès all;
Thank Love, that list you to his mercy call."

When they this song had sung a little thraw,
They stent awhile, and therewith unaffrayed,
As I beheld and cast mine eyne alaw,
From bough to bough they hippèd, and they
  played,
And freshly in their birdès kind arrayed

Their feathers new, and fret them in the sun,
And thankèd Love that han their matès won.

James I of Scotland (1394–1437)

A Catch

I have a pretty titmouse
Come pecking on my toe.
Gossip, with you I purpose
To drink before I go.
Little pretty nightingale,
Among the branches green,
Give us of your Christmas ale,
In the honour of Saint Stephen.
Robin Redbreast with his notes
Singing aloft in the quire,
Warneth to get you frieze coats,
For Winter then draweth near.
My bridle lieth on the shelf,
If you will have any more,
Vouchsafe to sing it yourself,
For here you have all my store.

William Wager (fl. 1566)

The Nightingale

The nightingale, as soon as April bringeth
  Unto her rested sense a perfect waking,
While late-bare earth, proud of new clothing,
  springeth,
    Sings out her woes, a thorn her song-book
    making;
      And mournfully bewailing,
      Her throat in tunes expresseth
      What grief her breast oppresseth
For Tereus' force on her chaste will prevailing.

O Philomela fair, O take some gladness
That here is juster cause of plaintful sadness:
  Thine earth now springs, mine fadeth;
Thy thorn without, my thorn my heart
  invadeth.

Alas, she hath no other cause of anguish
  But Tereus' love, on her by strong hand
    wroken,
Wherein she suffering, all her spirits languish,
  Full womanlike complains her will was
    broken.

But I, who, daily craving,
   Cannot have to content me,
   Have more cause to lament me,
Since wanting is more woe than too much
   having.

O Philomela fair, O take some gladness
That here is juster cause of plaintful sadness:
   Thine earth now springs, mine fadeth;
Thy thorn without, my thorn my heart
   invadeth.

Sir Philip Sidney (1554–1586)

Spring

Spring, the sweet Spring, is the year's pleasant
    king;
Then blooms each thing, then maids dance in
    a ring;
Cold doth not sting, the pretty birds do sing,
Cuckoo, jug-jug, pu-we, to-witta-woo!

The palm and the may make country houses
    gay;
Lambs frisk and play, the shepherds pipe all
    day;
And we hear aye birds tune this merry lay,
Cuckoo, jug-jug, pu-we, to-witta-woo.

The fields breathe sweet, the daisies kiss our
    feet;
Young lovers meet, old wives a-sunning sit;
In every street these tunes our ears do greet,
Cuckoo, jug-jug, pu-we, to-witta-woo.
    Spring, the sweet Spring.

Thomas Nashe (1567–1601)

A Bird Committee

The cushat crouds, the corbie cries,
The cuckoo couks, the prattling pyes
   To geck there they begin;
The jargon of the jangling jays,
The craiking craws and keekling kays,
   They deave't me with their din.
The painted pawn with Argus eyes
   Can on his May-cock call;
The turtle wails on withered trees,
   And Echo answers all,
     Repeating, with greeting,
     How fair Narcissus fell,
     By lying and spying
     His shadow in the well.

Alexander Montgomerie (c. 1550–1600)

The Ousel-Cock so Black of Hue

The ousel-cock, so black of hue,
   With orange-tawny bill,
The throstle with his note so true,
   The wren with little quill;
The finch, the sparrow, and the lark,
   The plain-song cuckoo grey,
Whose note full many a man doth mark,
   And dares not answer nay.

William Shakespeare (1564–1616)

Spring and Winter

When daisies pied, and violets blue,
   And lady-smocks all silver-white
And cuckoo-buds of yellow hue
   Do paint the meadows with delight,
The cuckoo then, on every tree,
Mocks married men, for thus sings he,
      Cuckoo;
Cuckoo, cuckoo,—O word of fear,
Unpleasing to a married ear!
When shepherds pipe on oaten straws,
   And merry larks are ploughmen's clocks,
When turtles tread, and rooks, and daws,
   And maidens bleach their summer smocks,
The cuckoo then, on every tree, etc., etc.

When icicles hang by the wall,
   And Dick the shepherd blows his nail,
And Tom bears logs into the hall,
   And milk comes frozen home in pail,
When blood is nipped, and ways be foul,
Then nightly sings the staring owl,
      To-whit;
   To-who, a merry note,

While greasy Joan doth keel the pot.
When all around the wind doth blow,
    And coughing drowns the parson's saw,
And birds sit brooding in the snow,
    And Marian's nose looks red and raw,
When roasted crabs hiss in the bowl,
    Then nightly sings the staring owl, etc., etc.

William Shakespeare (1564–1616)

'Wilt thou be gone . . .'

Jul. Wilt thou be gone? it is not near day:
It was the nightingale, and not the lark,
That pierced the fearful hollow of thine ear;
Nightly she sings on yon pomegranate tree:
Believe me, love, it was the nightingale.

Rom. It was the lark, the herald of the morn,
No nightingale: look, love, what envious streaks
Do lace the severing clouds in yonder east:
Night's candles are burnt out, and jocund day
Stands tiptoe on the misty mountain tops:
I must be gone and live, or stay and die.

Jul. Yon light is not daylight, I know it, I:
It is some meteor that the sun exhales,
To be to thee this night a torch-bearer,
And light thee on thy way to Mantua:
Therefore stay yet; thou need'st not to be gone.

Rom. Let me be ta'en, let me be put to death;
I am content, so thou wilt have it so.

I'll say yon grey is not the morning's eye,
'Tis but the pale reflex of Cynthia's
    brow;
Nor that is not the lark, whose notes do
    beat
The vaulty heaven so high above our
    heads:
I have more care to stay than will to go:
Come, death, and welcome! Juliet wills
    it so.
How is't, my soul? let's talk; it is not day.

Jul. It is, it is; hie hence, be gone, away!
It is the lark that sings so out of tune,
Straining harsh discords and unpleasing
    sharps.
Some say the lark makes sweet division;
This doth not so, for she divideth us:
Some say the lark and loathèd toad
    change eyes;
O! now I would they had changed voices
    too,
Since arm from arm that voice doth us
    affray,
Hunting thee hence with hunts-up to
    the day.

O! now be gone; more light and light it
    grows.
Rom. More light and light; more dark and
    dark our woe.

William Shakespeare (1564–1616)

The Merry Month of May

O, the month of May, the merry month of May,
So frolic, so gay, and so green, so green, so
  green!
O, and then did I unto my true love say,
Sweet Peg, thou shalt be my Summer's Queen.

Now the nightingale, the pretty nightingale,
The sweetest singer in all the forest quire,
Entreats thee, sweet Peggy, to hear thy true
  love's tale:
Lo, yonder she sitteth, her breast against a
  brier.

But O, I spy the cuckoo, the cuckoo, the
  cuckoo;
See where she sitteth; come away, my joy:
Come away, I prithee, I do not like the cuckoo
Should sing where my Peggy and I kiss and
  toy.

O, the month of May, the merry month of May,
So frolic, so gay, and so green, so green, so
  green!
O, and then did I unto my true love say,
Sweet Peg, thou shalt be my Summer's Queen.

Thomas Dekker (1575–1641)

To Robin Redbreast

Led out for dead, let thy last kindness be
With leaves and moss-work for to cover me:
And while the wood-nymphs my cold corse
   inter,
Sing thou my dirge, sweet warbling chorister;
For epitaph in foliage next write this—
Here, here the tomb of Robin Herrick is.

Robert Herrick (1591–1674)

The Bird

Hither thou com'st: the busy wind all night
Blew through thy lodging, where thy own
   warm wing
Thy pillow was. Many a sullen storm
(For which course man seems much the fitter
   born,)
    Rain'd on thy bed
    And harmless head.

And now as fresh and cheerful as the light
Thy little heart in early hymns doth sing
Unto that Providence, whose unseen arm
Curb'd them, and clothed thee well and warm.
   All things that be praise him; and had
   Their lesson taught them, when first made.

So hills and valleys into singing break,
And though poor stones have neither speech
   nor tongue,
While active winds and streams both run and
   speak,
Yet stones are deep in admiration.

Thus Praise and Prayer here beneath the Sun
Make lesser mornings, when the great are
done.

For each inclosèd Spirit is a star
Inlightning his own little sphere,
Whose light, though fetcht and borrowed from
afar,
Both mornings makes, and evenings there.

Henry Vaughan (1621–1695)

The Armony of Byrdes

1

When Dame Flora
  In die aurora
Had covered the meadows with flowers,
And all the field
Was over distilled
  With lusty Aprell showers;

2

For my disport,
  Me to comfort,
When the day began to spring,
Forth I went
With a good intent,
  To hear the Byrdes sing.

3

I was not past
  Not a stone's cast
So nigh as I could deem;
But I did see
A goodly tree
  Within an arbour green.

4

Whereon did light
  Byrdes as thick
As stars in the sky;
Praising our Lord,
Without discord,
  With goodly armony.

5

Then sang the avis
  Called the mavis
The treble in ellamy,
That from the ground
Her notes around
  Were heard into the sky.

6

Then all the rest
  At her request,
Both mean, bass, and tenor,
With her did respond
This glorious sound:
  Te dominum confitemur.

7

Then said the nightingale,
  To make short tale,
For words I do refuse,
Because my delight
Both day and night
  Is singing for to use.

8

Then the Byrdes all
  Domesticall,
All at once did cry.
For mankind's sake,
Both early and late
  We be all ready to die.

9

Then the red brest
  His tunes redrest,
And said now will I hold
With the church, for there
Out of the air
  I keep me from the cold.

10

Then the eagle spake,
  Ye know my estate,
That I am lord and king;
Therefore will I
To the Father only
  Give laud and praising.

11

Then said the dove,
  Scripture doth prove
That from the deity
The holy spirit
In Christ did light
  In likeness of me.

12

Then said the wren,
  I am called the hen
Of our Lady most comely;
Then of her sun
My notes shall run
  For the love of that Lady.

13

The swallows sang sweet,
  To man we be meet;
For with him we do build,
Like as from above
God for mannes love
  Was born of a maiden mild.

14

Then in prostration
  They made oration
To Christ that died upon the rood;
To have mercy from those
For whom he chose
  To shed his precious blood.

15

With supplication
  They made intercession,
And sang Miserere nostri;
Rehearsing this text
In English next:
  Lord on us have mercy!

Anon.

Sweet Suffolk Owl

Sweet Suffolk owl, so trimly dight,
With feathers like a lady bright,
Thou singest alone, sitting by night,
   Te whit, te whoo, te whit, to whit.
Thy note, that forth so freely rolls,
With shrill command the mouse controls,
And sings a dirge for dying souls,
   Te whit, te whoo, te whit, to whit.

Anon.

The Bird that Bears the Bell

The nightingale, the organ of delight,
  The nimble lark, the blackbird, and the
    thrush,
And all the pretty quiristers of flight,
  That chant their music notes on every bush,
Let them no more contend who shall excel;
The cuckoo is the bird that bears the bell.

Anon.

Philip My Sparrow

Of all the birds that I do know,
   Philip my sparrow hath no peer;
For sit she high, or sit she low,
   Be she far off, or be she near,
There is no bird so fair, so fine,
   Nor yet so fresh as this of mine;
For when she once hath felt a fit,
   Philip will cry still: yet, yet, yet.

Come in a morning merrily
   When Philip hath been lately fed;
Or on an evening soberly
   When Philip list to go to bed;
It is a heaven to hear my Phipp,
   How she can chirp with merry lip,
For when she once hath felt a fit,
   Philip will cry still: yet, yet, yet.

She never wanders far abroad,
   But is at home when I do call.
If I command she lays on load
   With lips, with teeth, with tongue and all.
She chants, she chirps, she makes such cheer,

That I believe she hath no peer.
For when she once hath felt the fit,
   Philip will cry still: yet, yet, yet.

And yet besides all this good sport
   My Philip can both sing and dance,
With new found toys of sundry sort
   My Philip can both prick and prance.
And if you say but: fend cut, Phipp!
   Lord, how the peat will turn and skip!
For when she once hath felt the fit,
   Philip will cry still: yet, yet, yet.

And to tell truth he were to blame,
   Having so fine a bird as she,
To make him all this goodly game
   Without suspect or jealousy;
He were a churl and knew no good,
   Would see her faint for lack of food,
For when she once hath felt the fit,
   Philip will cry still: yet, yet, yet.

Anon.

Nursery Rhyme

Jenny Wren fell sick;
   Upon a merry time,
In came Robin Redbreast,
   And brought her sops and wine.

Eat well of the sop, Jenny,
   Drink well of the wine;
Thank you, Robin, kindly,
   You shall be mine.

Jenny she got well,
   And stood upon her feet,
And told Robin plainly
   She loved him not a bit.

Robin, being angry,
   Hopp'd on a twig,
Saying, Out upon you,
   Fye upon you, bold-faced jig!

Anon.

Cuckoo Lore

In April
  He shows his bill.
In May
  He sings all day.
In June
  He changes his tune.
In July
  He says good-bye.
In August
  Go he must.

Anon.

FROM THE RESTORATION TO THE
NINETEENTH CENTURY

The Barn Owl

While moonlight, silvering all the walls,
Through every mouldering crevice falls,
Tipping with white his powdery plume,
As shades or shifts the changing gloom;
The Owl that, watching in the barn,
Sees the mouse creeping in the corn,
Sits still and shuts his round blue eyes
As if he slept,—until he spies
The little beast within his stretch—
Then starts,—and seizes on the wretch!

Samuel Butler (1612–1680)

The Swallow

Departure

The swallow, privileged above the rest
Of all the birds as man's familiar guest,
Pursues the sun in summer, brisk and bold,
But wisely shuns the persecuting cold;
Is well to chancels and to chimneys known,
Though 'tis not thought she feeds on smoke
   alone.
From hence she has been held of heavenly
   line,
Endued with particles of soul divine:
This merry chorister had long possessed
Her summer seat, and feathered well her nest,
Till frowning skies began to change their cheer,
And time turned up the wrong side of the year;
The shedding trees began the ground to strow
With yellow leaves, and bitter blast to blow;
Sad auguries of winter thence she drew,
Which by instinct or prophecy she knew;
When prudence warned her to remove
   betimes,
And seek a better heaven and warmer climes.

Her sons were summoned on a steeple's
    height,
And, called in common council, vote a flight.
The day was named, the next that should be
    fair;
All to the general rendezvous repair;
They try their fluttering wings, and trust
    themselves in air.

Return

Who but the swallow now triumphs alone?
The canopy of heaven is all her own:
Her youthful offspring to their haunts repair,
And glide along in glades, and skim in air,
And dip for insects in the purling springs,
And stoop on rivers, to refresh their wings.
Their mothers think a fair provision made,
That every son can live upon his trade:
And, now the careful charge is off their hands,
Look out for husbands, and new nuptial
    bands:
The youthful widow longs to be supplied;
But first the lover is by lawyers tied
To settle jointure-chimneys on the bride.
So thick they couple, in so short a space,

That Martin's marriage-offerings rise apace.
Their ancient houses, running to decay,
Are furbished up, and cèmented with clay;
They teem already; stores of eggs are laid,
And brooding mothers call Lucina's aid.

John Dryden (1631–1700)

The Sparrow and Diamond

I lately saw, what now I sing,
   Fair Lucia's hand display'd;
The finger grac'd a diamond ring,
   On that a sparrow play'd.

The feather'd play-thing she caressed,
   She stroked its head and wings;
And while it nestled on her breast,
   She lisped the dearest things.

With chisell'd bill a spark ill-set
   He loosened from the rest,
And swallowed down to grind his meat,
   The easier to digest.

She seized his bill with wild affright,
   Her diamond to descry:
'Twas gone! she sickened at the sight,
   Moaning her bird would die.

The tongue-tied knocker none might use,
   The curtains none undraw,

The footmen went without their shoes,
   The street was laid with straw.

The doctor used his oily art
   Of strong emetic kind,
Th' apothecary played his part,
   And engineered behind.

When physic ceased to spend its store,
   To bring away the stone,
Dicky, like people given o'er,
   Picks up when let alone.

His eyes dispelled their sickly dews,
   He pecked behind his wing,
Lucia, recovering at the news,
   Relapses for the ring.

Meanwhile within her beauteous breast
   Two different passions strove;
When av'rice ended the contest,
   And triumphed over love.

Poor, little, pretty, fluttering thing,
   Thy pains the sex display,

Who, only to repair a ring,
  Could take thy life away.

Drive av'rice from your hearts, ye fair,
  Monster of foulest mien:
Ye would not let it harbour there,
  Could but its form be seen.

It made a virgin put on guile,
  Truth's image break her word,
A Lucia's face forbear to smile,
  A Venus kill her bird.

Matthew Green (1696–1737)

from Windsor Forest

See! from the brake the whirring pheasant
  springs,
And mounts exulting on triumphant wings;
Short in his joy, he feels the fiery wound,
Flutters in blood, and panting beats the
  ground.
Ah! what avail his glossy, varying dyes,
His purple crest, and scarlet-circled eyes,
The vivid green his shining plumes unfold,
His painted wings, and breast that flames with
  gold?

. . . . . .

With slaughtering guns the unwearied fowler
  roves,
When frosts have whitened all the naked
  groves;
Where doves in flocks the leafless trees
  o'ershade,
And lonely woodcocks haunt the watery glade.
He lifts the tube, and levels with his eye:
Straight a short thunder breaks the frozen sky.
Oft, as in airy rings they skim the heath,
The clamorous lapwings feel the leaden death:

Oft, as the mounting larks their notes prepare,
They fall, and leave their little lives in air.

Alexander Pope (1688–1744)

from Essay on Man

Has God, thou fool! work'd solely for thy good,
Thy joy, thy pastime, thy attire, thy food?

Is it for thee the lark ascends and sings?
Joy tunes his voice, joy elevates his wings.

Is it for thee the linnet pours his throat?
Loves of his own and raptures swell the note.

Is thine alone the seed that strews the plain?
The birds of heaven shall vindicate their grain.

Alexander Pope (1688–1744)

Ode to the Cuckoo

Hail, beauteous stranger of the grove!
Thou messenger of Spring!
Now Heaven repairs thy rural seat,
And woods thy welcome sing.

What time the daisy decks the green,
Thy certain voice we hear;
Hast thou a star to guide thy path,
Or mark the rolling year?

Delightful visitant! with thee
I hail the time of flowers,
And hear the sound of music sweet
From birds among the bowers.

The schoolboy, wandering through the wood
To pull the primrose gay,
Starts, the new voice of spring to hear,
And imitates thy lay.

What time the pea puts on the bloom,
Thou fliest thy vocal vale,
An annual guest in other lands,
Another spring to hail.

Sweet bird! thy bower is ever green,
Thy sky is ever clear;
Thou hast no sorrow in thy song,
No winter in thy year.

Oh, could I fly, I'd fly with thee!
We'd make, with joyful wing,
Our annual visit o'er the globe,
Companions of the spring.

Michael Bruce (1746–1767)

The Linnet

Within the bush, her covert nest
A little linnet fondly prest;
The dew sat chilly on her breast,
   Sae early in the morning.

She soon shall see her tender brood,
The pride, the pleasure of the wood,
Amang the fresh green leaves bedew'd
   Awake the early morning.

Robert Burns (1759–1796)

The Heather was Blooming

The heather was blooming, the meadows were
    mawn,
Our lads gaed a-hunting, ae day at the dawn,
O'er moors and o'er mosses and mony a glen;
At length they discover'd a bonnie moor-hen.

  I red you beware at the hunting, young men;
  I red you beware at the hunting, young men;
  Tak some on the wing, and some as they
    spring,
  But cannily steal on a bonnie moor-hen.

Sweet brushing the dew from the brown
    heather-bells,
Her colours betrayed her on yon mossy fells;
Her plumage outlustred the pride o' the
    spring,
And O! as she wanton'd gay on the wing.

Auld Phœbus himsel, as he peep'd o'er the hill,
In spite of her plumage he tried his skill:
He levell'd his rays where she bask'd on the brae—

His rays were outshone, and but mark'd where
  she lay.

They hunted the valley, they hunted the hill,
The best of our lads wi' the best of their skill;
But still as the fairest she sat in their sight,
Then whirr! she was over, a mile at a flight.

Robert Burns (1759–1796)

The Robin in Winter

No noise is here, or none that hinders thought.
The redbreast warbles still, but is content
With slender notes, and more than half
   suppressed:
Pleased with his solitude, and flitting light
From spray to spray, where'er he rest he shakes
From many a twig the pendent drops of ice,
That twinkle in the withered leaves below.
Stillness, accompanied with sounds so soft,
Charms more than silence.

William Cowper (1731–1800)

On a Goldfinch
(Starved to Death in his Cage)

Time was when I was free as air,
The thistles downy feed my fare,
   My drink the morning dew;
I perched at will on ev'ry spray,
My form genteel, my plumage gay,
   My strain for ever new.

But gaudy plumage, sprightly strain,
And form genteel were all in vain,
   And of a transient date;
For, caught and caged, and starved to death,
In dying sighs my little breath
   Soon passed the wiry grate.

Thanks, gentle swain, for all my woes,
And thanks for this effectual close
   And cure of ev'ry ill!
More cruelty could none express;
And I, if you had shewn me less,
   Had been your pris'ner still.

William Cowper (1731–1800)

The Jackdaw

There is a bird who, by his coat,
And by the hoarseness of his note,
  Might be supposed a crow;
A great frequenter of the church,
Where, bishop-like, he finds a perch,
  And dormitory too.

Above the steeple shines a plate,
That turns and turns, to indicate
  From what point blows the weather.
Look up—your brains begin to swim,
'Tis in the clouds—that pleases him,
  He chooses it the rather.

Fond of the speculative height,
Thither he wings his airy flight,
  And thence securely sees
The bustle and the raree-show
That occupy mankind below,
  Secure and at his ease.

You think, no doubt, he sits and muses
On future broken bones and bruises,

If he chances to fall.
No; not a single thought like that
Employs his philosophic pate,
   Or troubles it at all.

He sees, that this great roundabout—
The world, with all its motley rout,
   Church, army, physic, law,
Its customs, and its bus'nesses,
Is no concern at all of his,
   And says—what says he?—Caw.

Thrice happy bird! I too have seen
Much of the vanities of men;
   And sick of having seen 'em,
Would cheerfully these limbs resign
For such a pair of wings as thine
   And such a head between 'em.

William Cowper (1731–1800)

The Nightingale and the Glowworm

A Nightingale that all day long
Had cheered the village with his song,
Nor yet at eve his note suspended,
Nor yet when eventide was ended,
Began to feel, as well he might,
The keen demands of appetite;
When looking eagerly around,
He spied far off, upon the ground,
A something shining in the dark,
And knew the Glowworm by his spark;
So, stooping down from hawthorn top,
He thought to put him in his crop.

The worm, aware of his intent,
Harangued him thus, right eloquent:
"Did you admire my lamp," quoth he,
"As much as I your minstrelsy,
You would abhor to do me wrong,
As much as I to spoil your song:
For 'twas the self-same Power Divine
Taught you to sing, and me to shine;
That you with music, I with light,
Might beautify and cheer the night."
The songster heard this short oration,

And warbling out his approbation,
Released him, as my story tells,
And found a supper somewhere else.

William Cowper (1731–1800)

A Bird's Nest

It was my admiration
To view the structure of that little work,
A bird's nest—mark it well, within, without:
No tool had he that wrought, no knife to cut,
No rail to fix, no bodkin to insert,
No glue to join; his little beak was all;
And yet how neatly finished! What nice hand,
With every implement and means of art,
And twenty years' apprenticeship to boot,
Could make me such another? Fondly then
We boast of excellence, whose noblest skill
Instinctive genius foils!

James Hurdis (1763–1801)

A Storm on the East Coast

View now the winter storm! above, one cloud,
Black and unbroken, all the skies o'ershroud:
The unwieldy porpoise through the day before
Had rolled in view of boding men on shore;
And sometimes hid and sometimes showed his
    form,
Dark as the cloud and furious as the storm.
All where the eye delights yet dreads to roam,
The breaking billows cast the flying foam
Upon the billows rising—all the deep
Is restless change; the waves so swelled and
    steep,
Breaking and sinking, and the sunken swells,
Nor one, one moment, in its station dwells:
But nearer land you may the billows trace,
As if contending in their watery chase;
May watch the mightiest till the shoal they
    reach,
Then break and hurry to their utmost stretch;
Curled as they come, they strike with furious
    force,
And then reflowing, take their grating course,
Raking the rounded flints, which ages past

Rolled by their rage, and shall to ages last.
Far off the petrel in the troubled way
Swims with her brood, or flutters in the spray;
She rises often, often drops again,
And sports at ease on the tempestuous main.
High o'er the restless deep, above the reach
Of gunners' hope, vast flocks of wild-duck
    stretch;
Far as the eye can glance on either side,
In a broad space and level line they glide;
All in their wedge-like figures from the north
Day after day, flight after flight, go forth.
In-shore their passage tribes of sea-gulls urge,
And drop for prey within the sweeping surge;
Oft in the rough opposing blast they fly
Far back, then turn and all their force apply,
While to the storm they give their weak
    complaining cry;
Or clap the sleek white pinion on the breast,
And in the restless ocean dip for rest.

George Crabbe (1754–1832)

Pigeon and Wren

Coo-oo, coo-oo,
It's as much as a pigeon can do
    To maintain two;
But the little wren can maintain ten,
And bring them all up like gentlemen.

Anon.

Crows

On the first of March,
The craws begin to search.
By the first of April,
They are sitting still.
By the first o' May
They're a flown away;
Croupin' greedy back again,
Wi' October's wind and rain.

Anon.

Magpies

One, Sorrow,
Two, Mirth,
Three, a Wedding,
Four, a Birth,
Five, for Silver,
Six, for Gold,
Seven, for a secret not to be told,
Eight, for Heaven,
Nine, for Hell,
And Ten, for the devil's ain sel.

Anon.

FROM THE NINETEENTH TO THE TWENTIETH CENTURY

The Blossom

Merry, merry sparrow!
  Under leaves so green,
A happy blossom
  Sees you, swift as arrow,
Seek your cradle narrow
  Near my bosom.

Pretty, pretty robin!
  Under leaves so green,
A happy blossom
  Hears you sobbing, sobbing,
Pretty, pretty robin,
  Near my bosom.

William Blake (1757–1827)

The Birds

He.   Where thou dwellest, in what grove,
      Tell me, fair one, tell me, love;
    Where thou thy charming nest dost build,
      O thou pride of every field!

She.   Yonder stands a lonely tree,
      There I live and mourn for thee;
    Morning drinks my silent tear,
      And evening winds my sorrow bear.

He.   O thou summer's harmony,
      I have liv'd and mourn'd for thee;
    Each day I mourn along the wood,
      And night hath heard my sorrows loud.

She.   Dost thou truly long for me?
      And am I thus sweet to thee?
    Sorrow now is at an end,
      O my lover and my friend!

He.   Come, on wings of joy we'll fly
        To where my bower hangs on high;
    Come, and make thy calm retreat
        Among green leaves and blossoms
        sweet.

                William Blake (1757–1827)

Song

Love and harmony combine,
And around our souls entwine,
While thy branches mix with mine,
And our roots together join.

Joys upon our branches sit,
Chirping loud and singing sweet;
Like gentle streams beneath our feet
Innocence and virtue meet.

Thou the golden fruit dost bear,
I am clad in flowers fair;
Thy sweet boughs perfume the air,
And the turtle buildeth there.

There she sits and feeds her young,
Sweet I hear her mournful song;
And thy lovely leaves among,
There is love, I hear her tongue.

There his charming nest doth lay,
There he sleeps the night away,

There he sports along the day,
And doth among our branches play.

William Blake (1757–1827)

Ode to a Nightingale

My heart aches, and a drowsy numbness pains
  My sense, as though of hemlock I had drunk,
Or emptied some dull opiate to the drains
  One minute past, and Lethe-wards had sunk:
'Tis not through envy of thy happy lot,
  But being too happy in thy happiness,—
      That thou, light-wingèd dryad of the trees,
        In some melodious plot
    Of beechen green, and shadows
      numberless,
      Singest of summer in full-throated ease.

O for a draught of vintage! that hath been
  Cool'd a long age in the deep-delvèd earth,
Tasting of Flora and the country-green,
  Dance, and Provençal song, and sunburnt
    mirth!
O for a beaker full of the warm South!
  Full of the true, the blushful Hippocrene,
      With beaded bubbles winking at the brim,
        And purple-stainèd mouth;

That I might drink, and leave the world
    unseen,
        And with thee fade away into the forest
        dim:

Fade far away, dissolve, and quite forget
    What thou among the leaves hast never
        known,
The weariness, the fever, and the fret
    Here, where men sit and hear each other
        groan;
Where palsy shakes a few, sad, last, grey hairs,
    Where youth grows pale, and spectre-thin,
        and dies;
    Where but to think is to be full of sorrow
        And leaden-eyed despairs;
    Where Beauty cannot keep her lustrous eyes,
        Or new Love pine at them beyond
        to-morrow.

Away! away! for I will fly to thee,
    Not charioted by Bacchus and his pards,
But on the viewless wings of Poesy,
    Though the dull brain perplexes and retards:
Already with thee! tender is the night,

And haply the Queen-Moon is on her throne,
  Cluster'd around by all her starry Fays;
    But here there is no light,
Save what from Heaven is with the breezes
  blown
    Through verdurous glooms and winding
      mossy ways.

I cannot see what flowers are at my feet,
  Nor what soft incense hangs upon the
    boughs,
But, in embalmèd darkness, guess each sweet
  Wherewith the seasonable month endows
The grass, the thicket, and the fruit-tree wild;
  White hawthorn, and the pastoral eglantine;
    Fast-fading violets cover'd up in leaves;
      And mid-May's eldest child,
    The coming musk-rose, full of dewy wine,
      The murmurous haunt of flies on
        summer eves.

Darkling I listen; and for many a time
  I have been half in love with easeful Death,
Call'd him soft names in many a musèd rhyme,
  To take into the air my quiet breath;

Now more than ever seems it rich to die,
  To cease upon the midnight with no pain,
  While thou art pouring forth thy soul abroad
      In such an ecstasy!
  Still wouldst thou sing, and I have ears in vain—
  To thy high requiem become a sod.

Thou wast not born for death, immortal Bird!
  No hungry generations tread thee down;
The voice I hear this passing night was heard
  In ancient days by emperor and clown:
Perhaps the self-same song that found a path
  Through the sad heart of Ruth, when, sick
    for home,
      She stood in tears amid the alien corn;
          The same that oft-times hath
      Charm'd magic casements, opening on
        the foam
      Of perilous seas, in faery lands forlorn.

Forlorn! the very word is like a bell
  To toll me back from thee to my sole self!
Adieu! the fancy cannot cheat so well
  As she is famed to do, deceiving elf.
Adieu! adieu! thy plaintive anthem fades

Past the near meadows, over the still stream,
  Up the hill-side; and now 'tis buried deep
    In the next valley-glades:
  Was it a vision, or a waking dream?
    Fled is that music:—Do I wake or sleep?

John Keats (1795–1821)

Epistle to Charles Cowden Clarke

Oft have you seen a swan superbly frowning,
And with proud breast his own white shadow
   crowning;
He slants his neck beneath the waters bright
So silently, it seems a beam of light
Come from the galaxy: anon he sports,—
With outspread wings the Naiad Zephyr
   courts,
Or ruffles all the surface of the lake
In striving from its crystal face to take
Some diamond water drops, and them to
   treasure
In milky nest and sip them off at leisure.
But not a moment can he there ensure them,
Nor to such downy rest can he allure them;
For down they rush as though they would be
   free,
And drop like hours into eternity.

John Keats (1795–1821)

'Say, doth the dull soil . . .'

Say, doth the dull soil
Quarrel with the proud forests it hath fed,
And feedeth still, more comely than itself?
Can it deny the chiefdom of green groves?
Or shall the tree be envious of the dove
Because it cooeth, and hath snowy wings
To wander wherewithal and find its joys?
We are such forest trees, and our fair boughs
Have bred forth, not pale solitary doves,
But eagles golden-feathered, who do tower
Above us in their beauty, and must reign
In right thereof; for 'tis the eternal law
That first in beauty should be first in might.

John Keats (1795–1821)

Goldfinches

Sometimes goldfinches one by one will drop
From low-hung branches: little space they stop;
But sip, and twitter, and their feathers sleek;
Then off at once, as in a wanton freak:
Or perhaps, to show their black and golden
   wings,
Pausing upon their yellow flutterings.

John Keats (1795–1821)

The Captive Bird

Poor captive bird! who, from thy narrow
    cage,
Pourest such music, that it might assuage
The rugged hearts of those who prisoned thee,
Were they not deaf to all sweet melody;
This song shall be thy rose: its petals pale
Are dead, indeed, my adored nightingale!
But soft and fragrant is the faded blossom,
And it has no thorn left to wound thy bosom.
   High, spirit-wingèd Heart! who dost for ever
Beat thine unfeeling bars with vain endeavour,
Till those bright plumes of thought, in which
    arrayed,
It over-soared this low and worldly shade,
Lie shattered; and thy panting, wounded
    breast
Stains with dear blood its unmaternal nest!
I weep vain tears: blood would less bitter be,
Yet poured forth gladlier, could it profit thee.

Percy Bysshe Shelley (1792–1822)

The Widow Bird

A widow bird sat mourning for her love
   Upon a wintry bough;
The frozen wind crept on above,
   The freezing stream below.

There was no leaf upon the forest bare,
   No flower upon the ground,
And little motion in the air,
   Except the mill-wheel sound.

Percy Bysshe Shelley (1792–1822)

Kingfishers

I cannot tell my joy, when o'er a lake
Upon a drooping bough with nightshade
  twined,
I saw two azure halcyons clinging downward
And thinning one bright bunch of amber
  berries,
With quick long beaks, and in the deep
  there lay
Those lovely forms imaged as in a sky.

Percy Bysshe Shelley (1792–1822)

Glycine's Song

A sunny shaft did I behold,
  From sky to earth it slanted:
And poised therein a bird so bold—
  Sweet bird, thou wert enchanted!
He sunk, he rose, he twinkled, he trolled
  Within that shaft of sunny mist;
His eyes of fire, his beak of gold,
  All else of amethyst!

And thus he sang: "Adieu! adieu!
  Love's dreams prove seldom true.
    Sweet month of May,
      We must away:
        Far, far away!
          To-day! to-day!"

Samuel Taylor Coleridge (1772–1834)

The Rime of the Ancient Mariner

Part the First

It is an ancient Mariner,
And he stoppeth one of three.
"By thy long grey beard and glittering eye,
Now wherefore stopp'st thou me?

"The Bridegroom's doors are opened wide,
And I am next of kin;
The guests are met, the feast is set:
May'st hear the merry din."

He holds him with his skinny hand,
"There was a ship," quoth he.
"Hold off! unhand me, greybeard loon!"
Eftsoons his hand dropt he.

He holds him with his glittering eye—
The Wedding-Guest stood still,
And listens like a three-years child:
The Mariner hath his will.

The Wedding-Guest sat on a stone;
He cannot choose but hear;
And thus spake on that ancient man,
The bright-eyed Mariner.

The ship was cheered, the harbour cleared,
Merrily did we drop
Below the kirk, below the hill,
Below the lighthouse top.

The Sun came up upon the left,
Out of the sea came he!
And he shone bright, and on the right
Went down into the sea.

Higher and higher every day,
Till over the mast at noon—
The Wedding-Guest here beat his breast,
For he heard the loud bassoon.

The bride hath paced into the hall,
Red as a rose is she;
Nodding their heads before her goes
The merry minstrelsy.

The Wedding-Guest he beat his breast,
Yet he cannot choose but hear;
And thus spake on that ancient man,
The bright-eyed Mariner.

"And now the Storm-blast came, and he
Was tyrannous and strong:
He struck with his o'ertaking wings,
And chased us south along.

With sloping masts and dipping prow,
As who pursued with yell and blow
Still treads the shadow of his foe

And forward bends his head,
The ship drove fast, loud roared the blast,
And southward aye we fled.

And now there came both mist and snow,
And it grew wondrous cold:
And ice, mast-high, came floating by,
As green as emerald.

And through the drifts the snowy clifts
Did send a dismal sheen:

For shapes of men nor beasts we ken—
The ice was all between.

The ice was here, the ice was there,
The ice was all around:
It cracked and growled, and roared and
    howled,
Like noises in a swound!

At length did cross an Albatross,
Through the fog it came;
As if it had been a Christian soul,
We hailed it in God's name.

It ate the food it ne'er had eat,
And round and round it flew.
The ice did split with a thunder-fit;
The helmsman steered us through!

And a good south wind sprung up behind;
The Albatross did follow,
And every day, for food or play,
Came to the mariners' hollo!

In mist or cloud, on mast or shroud,
It perched for vespers nine;
Whiles all the night, through fog-smoke white,
Glimmered the white Moon-shine."

"God save thee, ancient Mariner,
From the fiends, that plague thee thus!—
Why look'st thou so?"—"With my cross-bow
I shot the Albatross.

Part the Second

"The Sun now rose upon the right:
Out of the sea came he,
Still hid in mist, and on the left
Went down into the sea.

And the good south wind still blew behind,
But no sweet bird did follow,
Nor any day, for food or play,
Came to the mariners' hollo!

And I had done an hellish thing,
And it would work 'em woe:
For all averred I had killed the bird
That made the breeze to blow.

Ah, wretch! said they, the bird to slay,
That made the breeze to blow.

Nor dim nor red, like God's own head,
The glorious Sun uprist:
Then all averred I had killed the bird
That brought the fog and mist.
'Twas right, said they, such birds to slay,
That bring the fog and mist.

The fair breeze blew, the white foam flew,
The furrow followed free:
We were the first that ever burst
Into that silent sea.

Down dropt the breeze, the sails dropt down,
'Twas sad as sad could be;
And we did speak only to break
The silence of the sea!

All in a hot and copper sky,
The bloody Sun, at noon,
Right up above the mast did stand,
No bigger than the Moon.

Day after day, day after day,
We stuck, nor breath nor motion;
As idle as a painted ship
Upon a painted ocean.

Water, water, everywhere,
And all the boards did shrink;
Water, water, everywhere,
Nor any drop to drink.

The very deep did rot: O Christ!
That ever this should be!
Yea, slimy things did crawl with legs
Upon the slimy sea.

About, about, in reel and rout
The death-fires danced at night;
The water, like a witch's oils,
Burnt green, and blue, and white.

And some in dreams assurèd were
Of the Spirit that plagued us so:
Nine fathom deep he had followed us
From the land of mist and snow.

And every tongue, through utter drought,
Was withered at the root;
We could not speak, no more than if
We had been choked with soot.

Ah! well-a-day! what evil looks
Had I from old and young!
Instead of the cross, the Albatross
About my neck was hung.

Part the Third

"There passed a weary time. Each throat
Was parched, and glazed each eye.
A weary time! a weary time!
How glazed each weary eye!
When looking westward I beheld
A something in the sky.

At first it seemed a little speck,
And then it seemed a mist;
It moved and moved, and took at last
A certain shape, I wist.

A speck, a mist, a shape, I wist!
And still it neared and neared:

As if it dodged a water-sprite,
It plunged and tacked and veered.

With throats unslaked, with black lips baked,
We could not laugh nor wail;
Through utter drought all dumb we stood!
I bit my arm, I sucked the blood,
And cried, A sail! a sail!

With throats unslaked, with black lips baked,
Agape they heard me call:
Gramercy! they for joy did grin,
And all at once their breath drew in,
As they were drinking all.

See! see! (I cried) she tacks no more!
Hither to work us weal;
Without a breeze, without a tide,
She steadies with upright keel!

The western wave was all a-flame,
The day was well-nigh done!
Almost upon the western wave
Rested the broad, bright Sun;

When that strange shape drove suddenly
Betwixt us and the Sun.

And straight the Sun was flecked with bars
(Heaven's Mother send us grace!),
As if through a dungeon-grate he peered
With broad and burning face.

Alas! (thought I, and my heart beat loud),
How fast she nears and nears!
Are those her sails that glance in the Sun,
Like restless gossameres?

Are those her ribs through which the Sun
Did peer, as through a grate?
And is that Woman all her crew?
Is that a Death? and are there two?
Is Death that Woman's mate?

Her lips were red, her looks were free,
Her locks were yellow as gold:
Her skin was as white as leprosy,
The Night-Mare Life-in-Death was she,
Who thicks man's blood with cold.

The naked hulk alongside came,
And the twain were casting dice;
'The game is done! I've won! I've won!'
Quoth she, and whistles thrice.

The Sun's rim dips; the stars rush out;
At one stride comes the dark;
With far-heard whisper, o'er the sea,
Off shot the spectre-bark.

We listened and looked sideways up!
Fear at my heart, as at a cup,
My life-blood seemed to sip!
The stars were dim, and thick the night,
The steersman's face by his lamp gleamed
    white;
From the sails the dew did drip—
Till clomb above the eastern bar
The hornèd Moon, with one bright star
Within the nether tip.

One after one, by the star-dogged Moon,
Too quick for groan or sigh,
Each turned his face with a ghastly pang,
And cursed me with his eye.

Four times fifty living men
(And I heard nor sign nor groan),
With heavy thump, a lifeless lump,
They dropped down one by one.

The souls did from their bodies fly—
They fled to bliss or woe!
And every soul, it passed me by
Like the whizz of my cross-bow!"

Part the Fourth

"I fear thee, ancient Mariner!
I fear thy skinny hand!
And thou art long, and lank, and brown,
As is the ribbed sea-sand.

I fear thee, and thy glittering eye,
And thy skinny hand, so brown."—
"Fear not, fear not, thou Wedding-Guest!
This body dropt not down.

Alone, alone, all, all alone,
Alone on a wide, wide sea!
And never a saint took pity on
My soul in agony.

The many men, so beautiful!
And they all dead did lie;
And a thousand thousand slimy things
Lived on; and so did I.

I looked upon the rotting sea,
And drew my eyes away;
I looked upon the rotting deck,
And there the dead men lay.

I looked to heaven, and tried to pray;
But or ever a prayer had gusht,
A wicked whisper came, and made
My heart as dry as dust.

I closed my lids, and kept them close,
And the balls like pulses beat;
For the sky and the sea, and the sea and the
    sky,
Lay like a load on my weary eye,
And the dead were at my feet.

The cold sweat melted from their limbs,
Nor rot nor reek did they:

The look with which they looked on me
Had never passed away.

An orphan's curse would drag to hell
A spirit from on high;
But oh! more horrible than that
Is a curse in a dead man's eye!
Seven days, seven nights, I saw that curse,
And yet I could not die.

The moving Moon went up the sky,
And nowhere did abide;
Softly she was going up,
And a star or two beside—

Her beams bemocked the sultry main,
Like April hoar-frost spread;
But where the ship's huge shadow lay,
The charmèd water burnt alway
A still and awful red.

Beyond the shadow of the ship,
I watched the water-snakes:
They moved in tracks of shining white,

And when they reared, the elfish light
Fell off in hoary flakes.

Within the shadow of the ship
I watched their rich attire:
Blue, glossy green, and velvet black,
They coiled and swam; and every track
Was a flash of golden fire.

O happy living things! no tongue
Their beauty might declare:
A spring of love gushed from my heart,
And I blessed them unaware!
Sure my kind saint took pity on me,
And I blessed them unaware.

The selfsame moment I could pray;
And from my neck so free
The Albatross fell off, and sank
Like lead into the sea.

Part the Fifth

O! sleep it is a gentle thing,
Beloved from pole to pole!
To Mary Queen the praise be given!

She sent the gentle sleep from Heaven,
That slid into my soul.

The silly buckets on the deck,
That had so long remained,
I dreamt that they were filled with dew;
And when I awoke, it rained.

My lips were wet, my throat was cold,
My garments all were dank;
Sure I had drunken in my dreams,
And still my body drank.

I moved, and could not feel my limbs:
I was so light—almost
I thought that I had died in sleep,
And was a blessèd ghost.

And soon I heard a roaring wind:
It did not come anear;
But with its sound it shook the sails,
That were so thin and sere.

The upper air burst into life;
And a hundred fire-flags sheen;

To and fro they were hurried about!
And to and fro, and in and out,
The wan stars danced between.

And the coming wind did roar more loud,
And the sails did sigh like sedge;
And the rain poured down from one black
  cloud;
The Moon was at its edge.

The thick black cloud was cleft, and still
The Moon was at its side;
Like waters shot from some high crag,
The lightning fell with never a jag,
A river steep and wide.

The loud wind never reached the ship,
Yet now the ship moved on!
Beneath the lightning and the Moon
The dead men gave a groan.

They groaned, they stirred, they all uprose,
Nor spake, nor moved their eyes;
It had been strange, even in a dream,
To have seen those dead men rise.

The helmsman steered, the ship moved on;
Yet never a breeze up-blew;
The mariners all 'gan work the ropes,
Where they were wont to do;
They raised their limbs like lifeless tools—
We were a ghastly crew.

The body of my brother's son
Stood by me, knee to knee:
The body and I pulled at one rope,
But he said nought to me."

"I fear thee, ancient Mariner!"
"Be calm, thou Wedding-Guest!
'Twas not those souls that fled in pain,
Which to their corses came again,
But a troop of spirits blest:

For when it dawned—they dropped their arms
And clustered round the mast;
Sweet sounds rose slowly through their mouths,
And from their bodies passed.

Around, around, flew each sweet sound,
Then darted to the Sun;

Slowly the sounds came back again,
Now mixed, now one by one.

Sometimes a-dropping from the sky
I heard the skylark sing;
Sometimes all little birds that are,
How they seemed to fill the sea and air
With their sweet jargoning!

And now 'twas like all instruments,
Now like a lonely flute;
And now it is an angel's song,
That makes the heavens be mute.

It ceased; yet still the sails made on
A pleasant noise till noon,
A noise like of a hidden brook
In the leafy month of June,
That to the sleeping woods all night
Singeth a quiet tune.

Till noon we quietly sailed on,
Yet never a breeze did breathe:
Slowly and smoothly went the ship,
Moved onward from beneath.

Under the keel nine fathom deep,
From the land of mist and snow,
The Spirit slid: and it was he
That made the ship to go.
The sails at noon left off their tune,
And the ship stood still also.

The Sun, right up above the mast,
Had fixed her to the ocean:
But in a minute she 'gan stir,
With a short uneasy motion—
Backwards and forwards half her length
With a short uneasy motion.

Then like a pawing horse let go,
She made a sudden bound:
It flung the blood into my head,
And I fell down in a swound.

How long in that same fit I lay,
I have not to declare;
But ere my living life returned,
I heard, and in my soul discerned
Two voices in the air.

'Is it he?' quoth one, 'Is this the man?
By Him who died on cross,
With his cruel bow he laid full low
The harmless Albatross.

The spirit who bideth by himself
In the land of mist and snow,
He loved the bird that loved the man
Who shot him with his bow.'

The other was a softer voice,
As soft as honey-dew:
Quoth he, 'The man hath penance done,
And penance more will do.'

Part the Sixth
[...]

I woke, and we were sailing on
As in a gentle weather:
'Twas night, calm night, the Moon was high;
The dead men stood together.

All stood together on the deck,
For a charnel-dungeon fitter:

All fixed on me their stony eyes,
That in the Moon did glitter.

The pang, the curse, with which they died,
Had never passed away:
I could not draw my eyes from theirs,
Nor turn them up to pray.

And now this spell was snapt: once more
I viewed the ocean green,
And looked far forth, yet little saw
Of what had else been seen—

Like one, that on a lonesome road
Doth walk in fear and dread,
And having once turned round, walks on
And turns no more his head;
Because he knows a frightful fiend
Doth close behind him tread.

But soon there breathed a wind on me,
Nor sound nor motion made:
Its path was not upon the sea,
In ripple or in shade.

It raised my hair, it fanned my cheek
Like a meadow-gale of spring—
It mingled strangely with my fears,
Yet it felt like a welcoming.

Swiftly, swiftly flew the ship,
Yet she sailed softly too:
Sweetly, sweetly blew the breeze—
On me alone it blew.

Oh! dream of joy! is this indeed
The lighthouse top I see?
Is this the hill? is this the kirk?
Is this mine own countree?

[...]

And the bay was white with silent light,
Till rising from the same,
Full many shapes, that shadows were,
In crimson colours came.

A little distance from the prow
Those crimson shadows were:
I turned my eyes upon the deck—
Oh, Christ! what saw I there!

Each corse lay flat, lifeless and flat,
And, by the holy rood!
A man all light, a seraph-man,
On every corse there stood.

This seraph-band, each waved his hand:
It was a heavenly sight!
They stood as signals to the land,
Each one a lovely light:

This seraph-band, each waved his hand,
No voice did they impart—
No voice; but O, the silence sank
Like music on my heart.

But soon I heard the dash of oars,
I heard the Pilot's cheer;
My head was turned perforce away,
And I saw a boat appear.

The Pilot, and the Pilot's boy,
I heard them coming fast:
Dear Lord in Heaven! it was a joy
The dead men could not blast.

I saw a third—I heard his voice:
It is the Hermit good!
He singeth loud his godly hymns
That he makes in the wood.
He'll shrieve my soul, he'll wash away
The Albatross's blood.

Part the Seventh
[...]

Since then, at an uncertain hour,
That agony returns;
And till my ghastly tale is told,
This heart within me burns.

I pass, like night, from land to land;
I have strange power of speech;
That moment that his face I see,
I know the man that must hear me:
To him my tale I teach.

[...]

Farewell, farewell! but this I tell
To thee, thou Wedding-Guest!
He prayeth well, who loveth well
Both man and bird and beast.

He prayeth best, who loveth best
All things both great and small;
For the dear God who loveth us,
He made and loveth all."

The Mariner, whose eye is bright,
Whose beard with age is hoar,
Is gone: and now the Wedding-Guest
Turned from the bridegroom's door.

He went like one that hath been stunned,
And is of sense forlorn:
A sadder and a wiser man,
He rose the morrow morn.

Samuel Taylor Coleridge (1772–1834)

To the Cuckoo

O blithe new-comer! I have heard,
  I hear thee and rejoice:
O Cuckoo! shall I call thee bird,
  Or but a wandering Voice?

When I am lying on the grass,
  Thy twofold shout I hear;
From hill to hill it seems to pass,
  At once far off and near.

Though babbling only to the vale
  Of sunshine and of flowers,
Thou bringest unto me a tale
  Of visionary hours.

Thrice welcome, darling of the Spring!
  Even yet thou art to me
No bird, but an invisible thing,
  A voice, a mystery;

The same whom in my school-boy days
  I listened to; that Cry

Which made me look a thousand ways
   In bush, and tree, and sky.

To seek thee did I often rove
   Through woods and on the green;
And thou wert still a hope, a love;
   Still longed for, never seen!

And I can listen to thee yet;
   Can lie upon the plain
And listen, till I do beget
   That golden time again.

O blessèd bird! the earth we pace
   Again appears to be
An unsubstantial, fairy place
   That is fit home for thee!

William Wordsworth (1770–1850)

To the Skylark

Ethereal minstrel! pilgrim of the sky!
Dost thou despise the earth where cares
  abound?
Or while the wings aspire, are heart and eye
Both with thy nest upon the dewy ground?
Thy nest which thou canst drop into at will,
Those quivering wings composed, that music
  still!

To the last point of vision and beyond
Mount, daring warbler!—that love-prompted
  strain
'Twixt thee and thine a never failing bond—
Thrills not the less the bosom of the plain:
Yet might'st thou seem, proud privilege! to
  sing
All independent of the leafy Spring.

Leave to the nightingale her shady wood;
A privacy of glorious light is thine,
Whence thou dost pour upon the world a
  flood
Of harmony, with instinct more divine;

Type of the wise, who soar, but never roam—
True to the kindred points of Heaven and
   Home.

William Wordsworth (1770–1850)

Water Fowl

Mark how the feathered tenants of the flood,
With grace of motion that might scarcely seem
Inferior to the angelical, prolong
Their curious pastime! shaping in mid air
(And sometimes with ambitious wing that
   soars
High as the level of the mountain tops)
A circuit ampler than the lakes beneath
Their own domain; but ever while intent
On tracing and retracing that large round,
Their jubilant activity evolves
Hundreds of curves and circles, to and fro,
Upward and downward, progress intricate
Yet unperplexed, as if one spirit swayed
Their undefatigable flight. 'Tis done!
Ten times or more, I fancied it had ceased;
But lo! the vanished company again
Ascending, they approach—I hear their wings
Faint, faint at first; and then an eager sound,
Past in a moment, and as faint again!
They tempt the sun to sport amid their
   plumes;
They tempt the water, or the gleaming ice

To show them a fair image;—'tis themselves,
Their own fair forms, upon the glimmering
  plain,
Painted more soft and fair as they descend
Almost to touch; then up again aloft,
Up with a sally and a flash of speed,
As if they scorned both resting-place and rest.

William Wordsworth (1770–1850)

Eagles

(Composed at Dunollie Castle in the Bay of Oban)

Dishonoured Rock and Ruin! that, by law
Tyrannic, keep the Bird of Jove embarred
Like a lone criminal whose life is spared.
Vexed is he, and screams loud. The last I saw
Was on the wing; stooping, he struck with awe
Man, bird and beast; then, with a consort
   paired,
From a bold headland, their loved eerie's guard,
Flew high above Atlantic waves, to draw
Light from the fountain of the setting sun.
Such was this Prisoner once; and, when his
   plumes
The sea-blast ruffles as the storm comes on,
Then, for a moment, he, in spirit resumes
His rank 'mong freeborn creatures that live
   free,
His power, his beauty, and his majesty.

William Wordsworth (1770–1850)

The Parrot

A parrot, from the Spanish main,
  Full young and early caged came o'er,
With bright wings to the bleak domain
  Of Mulla's shore.

To spicy groves where he had won
  His plumage of resplendent hue,
His native fruits, and skies, and sun,
  He bade adieu.

For these he changed the smoke of turf,
  A heathery land and misty sky,
And turned on rocks and raging surf
  His golden eye.

But petted in our climate cold,
  He lived and chattered many a day:
Until with age, from green and gold
  His wings grew grey.

At last when blind, and seeming dumb,
  He scolded, laughed, and spoke no more,

A Spanish stranger chanced to come
  To Mulla's shore;

He hailed the bird in Spanish speech,
  The bird in Spanish speech replied;
Flapped round the cage with joyous screech,
  Dropt down, and died.

Thomas Campbell (1777–1844)

Epitaph on a Robin Redbreast

Tread lightly here, for here, 'tis said,
When piping winds are hushed around,
A small note wakes from underground,
Where now his tiny bones are laid.
No more in lone or leafless groves,
With ruffled wing and faded breast,
His friendless, homeless spirit roves;
Gone to the world where birds are blest!
Where never cat glides o'er the green,
Or school-boy's giant form is seen;
But love, and joy, and smiling Spring
Inspire their little souls to sing.

Samuel Rogers (1763–1855)

The Raven

Once upon a midnight dreary, while I
    pondered, weak and weary,
Over many a quaint and curious volume of
    forgotten lore—
While I nodded, nearly napping, suddenly
    there came a tapping,
As of someone gently rapping, rapping at my
    chamber door.
"'Tis some visitor," I muttered, "tapping at
    my chamber door—
    Only this and nothing more."

Ah, distinctly I remember it was in the bleak
    December,
And each separate dying ember wrought its
    ghost upon the floor.
Eagerly I wished the morrow—vainly I had
    sought to borrow
From my books surcease of sorrow—sorrow
    for the lost Lenore—
For the rare and radiant maiden whom the
    angels name Lenore—
    Nameless here for evermore.

And the silken sad uncertain rustling of each
   purple curtain
Thrilled me—filled me with fantastic terrors
   never felt before:
So that now, to still the beating of my heart, I
   stood repeating,
"'Tis some visitor entreating entrance at my
   chamber door—
Some late visitor entreating entrance at my
   chamber door—
   This it is and nothing more."

Presently my soul grew stronger; hesitating
   then no longer,
"Sir," said I, "or Madam, truly your
   forgiveness I implore;
But the fact is I was napping, and so gently
   you came rapping,
And so faintly you came tapping, tapping at
   my chamber door,
That I scarce was sure I heard you——" Here
   I opened wide the door—
   Darkness there and nothing more.

Deep into that darkness peering, long I stood
there wondering, fearing,
Doubtless, dreaming dreams no mortal ever
dared to dream before;
But the silence was unbroken, and the stillness
gave no token,
And the only word there spoken was the
whispered word "Lenore!"—
Merely this and nothing more.

Back into the chamber turning, all my soul
within me burning,
Soon again I heard a tapping, something
louder than before.
"Surely," said I, "surely that is something at
my window lattice;
Let me see, then, what thereat is, and this
mystery explore—
Let my heart be still a moment, and this
mystery explore—'Tis the wind and nothing
more."

Open here I flung the shutter, when, with
many a flirt and flutter,

In there stepped a stately Raven of the saintly
  days of yore—
Not the least obeisance made he; not a minute
  stopped or stayed he;
But, with mien of lord or lady perched above
  my chamber door—
Perched upon a bust of Pallas just above my
  chamber door—
  Perched and sat and nothing more.

Then this ebony bird beguiling my sad fancy
  into smiling,
By the grave and stern decorum of the
  countenance it wore,
"Though thy crest be shorn and shaven,
  thou," I said, "art sure no craven,
Ghastly grim and ancient Raven, wandering
  from the nightly shore—
Tell me what thy lordly name is on the Night's
  Plutonian shore!"
  Quoth the Raven: "Nevermore."

Much I marvelled this ungainly fowl to hear
  discourse so plainly,

Though its answer little meaning—little
relevancy bore;
For we cannot help agreeing that no living
human being
Ever yet was blessed with seeing bird above his
chamber door—
Bird or beast upon the sculptured bust above
his chamber door,
With such name as "Nevermore."

But the Raven, sitting lonely on that placid
bust, spoke only
That one word, as if his soul in that one word
he did outpour.
Nothing further then he uttered; not a feather
then he fluttered—
Till I scarcely more than muttered, "Other
friends have flown before—
On the morrow *he* will leave me, as my hopes
have flown before!"
Then the bird said: "Nevermore."

Startled at the stillness broken by reply so
aptly spoken,

"Doubtless," said I. "What it utters is its only
   stock and store,
Caught from some unhappy master, whom
   unmerciful disaster
Followed fast and followed faster, till his songs
   one burden bore—
Till the dirges of his Hope that melancholy
   burden bore
   Of "Never—nevermore."

But the Raven still beguiling all my sad soul
   into smiling,
Straight I wheeled a cushioned seat in front of
   bird, and bust, and door;
Then, upon the velvet sinking, I betook myself
   to linking
Fancy unto fancy, thinking what this ominous
   bird of yore—
What this grim, ungainly, ghastly, gaunt, and
   ominous bird of yore
   Meant in croaking "Nevermore."

Thus I sat engaged in guessing, but no syllable
   expressing

To the fowl whose fiery eyes now burned into
   my bosom's core;
This and more I sat divining, with my head at
   ease reclining,
On the cushion's velvet lining that the
   lamplight gloated o'er,
But whose velvet violet lining with the
   lamplight gloating o'er,
   She shall press, ah, nevermore!

Then, methought, the air grew denser,
   perfumed from an unseen censer
Swung by seraphim whose footfalls tinkled on
   the tufted floor.
"Wretch," I cried, "thy God hath lent thee—
   by these angels he hath sent thee,
Respite—respite and nepenthe from thy
   memories of Lenore!
Quaff, oh quaff this kind nepenthe and forget
   this lost Lenore!"
   Quoth the Raven: "Nevermore."

"Prophet," said I, "thing of evil;—prophet
   still, if bird or devil!

Whether Tempter sent, or whether Tempest
tossed thee here ashore,
Desolate, yet all undaunted, on this desert
land enchanted—
On this home by Horror haunted—tell me
truly, I implore—
Is there—*is* there balm in Gilead?—tell me—
tell me, I implore!"
Quoth the Raven: "Nevermore."

"Prophet," said I, "thing of evil—prophet still,
if bird or devil!
By that Heaven that bends above us—by that
God we both adore—
Tell this soul with sorrow laden, if, within the
distant Aiden,
It shall clasp a sainted maiden, whom the
angels name 'Lenore'—
Clasp a rare and radiant maiden, whom the
angels name Lenore."
Quoth the Raven: "Nevermore."

"Be that word our sign of parting, bird or
fiend!" I shrieked, upstarting—

"Get thee back into the tempest, and the
    Night's Plutonian shore!
Leave no black plume as a token of that lie thy
    soul hath spoken!
Leave my loneliness unbroken!—quit the bust
    above my door!—
Take thy beak from out my heart, and take thy
    form from off my door!"
Quoth the Raven: "Nevermore."

And the Raven, never flitting, still is sitting,
    still is sitting
On the pallid bust of Pallas, just above my
    chamber door;
And his eyes have all the seeming of a demon's
    that is dreaming,
And the lamplight o'er him streaming, throws
    his shadow on the floor;
And my soul, from out that shadow that lies
    floating on the floor,
Shall be lifted—nevermore.

Edgar Allan Poe (1809–1849)

The Rape of the Nest

In early spring I watched two sparrows build,
And then their nest within the thickest hedge
Construct, two small dear mates within whose
    life
And love, foreshadowed and foreshadowing, I
Had some sweet underpart. And so at last
The little round blue eggs were laid, and her
    post
The mother brooding kept, while far and wide
He sought the food for both, or, weariness
Compelling her, he changed and kept his post
Within the nest, and she flew forth in turn.

One day, a schoolboy, or some other, came
And caught her, took the eggs, and tore the
    nest,
And went his way. Then, as I stood looking
Through gathering tears and sobs, all swiftly
    winged,
Food-bearing, came the lover back, and flew
Into the thickest hedge. How shall we say
How the sweet mate lost for ever, the ruined
    home,

And the hope of young, with all life's life and
    light
Quenched at a moment for ever, were to him?
For grief like this grows dumb, deeper than
    words,
And man and animal are only one.

Francis Adams (1862–1893)

The Thrush's Nest

Within a thick and spreading hawthorn bush
   That overhung a molehill large and round,
I heard from morn to morn a merry thrush
   Sing hymns to sunrise, and I drank the
   sound
With joy; and, often an intruding guest,
   I watched her secret toils from day to day—
How true she warped the moss, to form a
   nest,
   And modelled it within with wood and clay;
And by and by, like heath-bells gilt with dew,
   There lay her shining eggs, as bright as
   flowers,
Ink-spotted over shells of greeny blue;
   And there I witnessed in the sunny hours
A brood of nature's minstrels chirp and fly,
   Glad as the sunshine and the laughing sky.

John Clare (1793–1864)

Little Trotty Wagtail

Little trotty wagtail he went in the rain,
And tittering, tottering sideways he ne'er got
    straight again,
He stooped to get a worm, and looked up to
    get a fly,
And then he flew away ere his feathers they
    were dry.

Little trotty wagtail, he waddled in the mud,
And left his little footmarks, trample where he
    would.
He waddled in the water-pudge, and waggle
    went his tail
And chirrup up his wings to dry upon the
    garden rail.

Little trotty wagtail, you nimble all about,
And in the dimpling water-pudge you waddle
    in and out;
Your home is nigh at hand, and in the warm
    pig-stye,
So little Master Wagtail, I'll bid you a good-bye.

John Clare (1793–1864)

from Song's Eternity

Mighty songs that miss decay,
    What are they?
Crowds and cities pass away
    Like a day.
Books are out and books are read;
    What are they?
Years will lay them with the dead—
    Sigh, sigh;
Trifles unto nothing wed,
    They die.

Dreamers, mark the honey bee;
    Mark the tree
Where the blue cap "tootle tee"
    Sings a glee
Sung to Adam and to Eve—
    Here they be.
When floods covered every bough,
    Noah's ark
Heard that ballad, singing now;
    Hark, hark,

"Tootle tootle tootle tee"—
    Can it be
Pride and fame must shadows be?
    Come and see—
Every season own her own;
    Bird and bee
Sing creation's music on;
    Nature's glee
Is in every mood and tone
    Eternity.

John Clare (1793–1864)

The Firetail's Nest

"Tweet," pipes the robin as the cat creeps by
Her nestling young that in the elderns lie,
And then the bluecap tootles in its glee,
Picking the flies from orchard apple tree,
And "pink" the chaffinch cries its well-known
   strain,
Urging its kind to utter "pink" again,
While in a quiet mood hedgesparrows try
An inward stir of shadowed melody.
Around the rotten tree the firetail mourns
As the old hedger to his toil returns,
Chopping the grain to stop the gap close by
The hole where her blue eggs in safety lie.
Of everything that stirs she dreameth wrong
And pipes her "tweet tut" fears the whole day
   long.

John Clare (1793–1864)

Birds, Why Are Ye Silent?

Why are ye silent,
    Birds? Where do ye fly?
Winter's not violent,
    With such a Spring sky.
The wheatlands are green, snow and frost are
    away;
Birds, why are ye silent on such a sweet day?

By the slated pig-stye,
    The redbreast scarce whispers:
Where last Autumn's leaves lie,
    The hedgesparrow just lispers.
And why are the chaffinch and bullfinch so
    still,
While the sulphur primroses bedeck the wood
    hill?

The bright yellowhammers—
    Are strutting about,
All still, and none stammers
    A single note out.
From the hedge starts the blackbird, at
    brookside to drink:

I thought he'd have whistled, but he only said
   "prink."

   The tree-creeper hustles
      Up fir's rusty bark;
   All silent he bustles;
      We needn't say hark.
There's no song in the forest, in field or in
   wood,
Yet the sun gilds the grass as though come in
   for good.

   How bright the odd daisies
      Peep under the stubbs!
   How bright pilewort blazes
      Where ruddled sheep rubs
The old willow trunk by the side of the brook
Where soon for blue violets the children will
   look.

   By the cot green and mossy
      Feed sparrow and hen:
   On the ridge brown and glossy
      They chuck now and then.

The wren cocks his tail o'er his back by the
    stye,
Where his green bottle nest will be made by
    and by.

Here's bunches of chickweed,
    With small starry flowers,
Where redcaps oft pick seeds
    In hungry spring hours;
And bluecap and blackcap, in glossy spring
    coat,
Are a-peeping in buds without singing a note.

Why silent should birds be
    And sunshine so warm?
Larks hide where the herds be
    By cottage and farm.
If wild flowers were blooming and fully set in
    the spring,
May-be all the birdies would cheerfully sing.

John Clare (1793–1864)

Love's Constancy

The dove shall be a hawk in kind,
The cuckoo change its tune,
The nightingale at Christmas sing,
The fieldfare come in June,
Ere I do change my love for thee,
These things shall change as soon.

So keep your heart at ease, my love,
Nor waste a joy for me;
I'll ne'er prove false to thee, my love,
Till fish drown in the sea,
And birds forget to fly, my love,
And then I'll think of thee.

The redcock's wing may turn to grey,
The crow's to silver white,
The night itself may be for day,
And sunshine wake at night
Till then—and then I'll prove more true
Than nature, life, and light.

John Clare (1793–1864)

The Song of the Carrion Crow

My roost is the creaking gibbet's beam,
  Where the murderer's bones swing bleaching;
Where the chattering chain rings back again
  To the night-wind's desolate screeching.

To and fro, as the fierce gusts blow,
  Merrily rocked am I;
And I note with delight the traveller's fright,
  As he cowers and hastens by.

I have fluttered where secret work has been
  done,
  Wrought with a trusty blade;
But what did I care, whether foul or fair,
  If I shared the feast it made?

I plunged my beak in the marbling cheek,
  I perched on the clammy brow,
And a dainty treat was that fresh meat
  To the greedy Carrion Crow.

I have followed the traveller dragging on
  O'er the mountains long and cold:

For I knew at last he must sink in the blast,
   Though spirit was never so bold.

He fell, and slept like a fair young bride,
   In his winding sheet of snow;
And quickly his breast had a table guest
   In the hungry Carrion Crow.

Famine and Plague bring joy to me,
   For I love the harvest they yield;—
And the fairest sight I ever see
   Is the crimson battle-field.

Far and wide is my charnel range,
   And rich carousel I keep,
Till back I come to my gibbet's home,
   To be merrily rocked to sleep.

When the world shall be spread with tombless
   dead
   And darkness shroud all below,
What triumph and glee to the last will be
   For the sateless Carrion Crow!

Eliza Cook (1818–1889)

· 141 ·

Farewells from Paradise: Bird-Spirit

I am the nearest nightingale
That singeth in Eden after you;
And I am singing loud and true,
And sweet,—I do not fail.
I sit upon a cypress bough,
Close to the gate, and I fling my song
Over the gate and through the mail
Of the warden angels marshall'd strong,—
 Over the gate and after you!
 And the warden angels let it pass,
 Because the poor brown bird, alas,
 Sings in the garden, sweet and true.
And I build my song of high pure notes,
Note after note, height over height,
Till I strike the arch of the Infinite,
And I bridge abysmal agonies
With strong clear calms of harmonies,—
And something abides, and something floats,
In the song which I sing after you.
Fare ye well, farewell!
 The creature-sounds, no longer audible,
 Expire at Eden's door.
 Each footstep of your treading

Treads out some cadence which ye heard
    before.
Farewell! the birds of Eden
Ye shall hear nevermore.

Elizabeth Barrett Browning (1806–1861)

The Eagle's Journey

From this grey crag in ether islanded,
I once at dawn, before the dark was done,
Full east my solitary pinions spread,
Seeking the sunken sources of the sun.
Chill o'er me hung the icy heavens, all black
Behind their fretted webs of fluttering gold.
Beneath me growl'd the grey unbottomed sea,
Inwardly shuddering. O'er her monstrous back
With restless weary shrugs in rapid fold
Her many-wrinkled mantle shifted she;
And scraped her craggy bays, and fiercely flung
Their stones about, and scraped them back
    again;
Gnawing and licking with mad tooth and
    tongue
The granite guardians of her drear domain.
Faint in transparent twilight where I gazed,
Hover'd a far-off flakelet of firm land.
Barely chin-high above the waters raised,
Peered the pale forehead of that spectral
    strand.
Thither I winged my penetrative flight:
The phantom coast, uncoiling many a twist

Of ghostly cable, as a diver might,
Swam slowly out to meet me, moist with spray.
But, ere I reach'd it, like a witch, the night
Had melted, first into a mist
Of melancholy amethyst,
Then utterly away.
And all around me was the large clear light
And crystal calm of the capacious day.

Owen Meredith (1803–1873)

The Carrier-Dove

If you have a carrier-dove
    That can fly over land and sea;
And a message for your Love,
    "Lady, I love but thee!"

And this dove will never stir,
    But straight from her to you,
And straight from you to her;
    As you know and she knows too.

Will you first ensure, O sage,
    Your dove that never tires
With your message in a cage,
    Though a cage of golden wires?

Or will you fling your dove:
    "Fly, darling, without rest,
Over land and sea to my Love,
    And fold your wings in her breast?"

James Thomson (1834–1882)

The Lover and Birds

Within a budding grove,
  In April's ear sang every bird his best,
But not a song to pleasure my unrest
  Or touch the tears unwept of bitter love;
Some spake methought with pity, some as if in
    jest.
        To every word
        Of every bird
     I listened, or replied as it behove.

Screamed Chaffinch, "Sweet, sweet, sweet!
  Pretty lovey, come and meet me here!"
"Chaffinch," quoth I, "be dumb awhile, in fear
  Thy darling prove no better than a cheat,
And never come, or fly when wintry days
    appear."
        Yet from a twig,
        With voice so big
     The little fowl his utterance did repeat.

Then I, "The man forlorn
  Hears Earth send up a foolish noise aloft."
"And what'll *he* do? What'll *he* do?" scoffed

The Blackbird, standing in an ancient
thorn,
Then spread his sooty wings and flitted to the
croft,
      With cackling laugh;
      Whom I, being half
    Enraged, called after, giving back his
    scorn.

Worse mocked the Thrush, "Die! die!
   O, could he do it? Could he do it? Nay!
Be quick! be quick! Here, here, here!" (went
his lay)
   "Take heed! take heed!" then, "Why? why?
why? why? why?
See-ee now! see-ee now!" (he drawled)
   "Back! back! back! R-r-r-run away!"
      O thrush, be still!
      Or at thy will
    Seek some less sad interpreter than I.

"Air, air! blue air and white!
Whither I flee, whither, O whither, O whither
I flee!"
(Thus the Lark hurried, mounting from the lea)

"Hills, countries, many waters glittering
    bright
Whither I see, whither I see! deeper, deeper,
    deeper, whither I see, see, see!"
        "Gay Lark," I said,
        "The song that's bred
    In happy nest may well to heaven take
        flight."

    "There's something, something sad
I half remember"—piped a broken strain.
Well sung, sweet Robin! Robin sung again.
    "Spring's opening, cheerily, cheerily! be we
        glad!"
Which moved, I wist not why, me melancholy
    mad,
        Till now, grown meek,
        With wetted cheek,
    Most comforting and gentle thoughts I
        had.

                    William Allingham (1824–1889)

A Memory

Four ducks on a pond,
A grass-bank beyond,
A blue sky of spring,
White clouds on the wing:
What a little thing
To remember for years—
To remember with tears.

William Allingham (1824–1889)

Sunset Wings

1

To-night this sunset spreads two golden wings
    Cleaving the western sky;
Winged too with wind it is, and winnowings
Of birds; as if the day's last hour in rings
    Of strenuous flight must die.

2

Sun-steeped in fire, the homeward pinions
  sway
    Above the dovecote-tops;
And clouds of starlings, ere they rest with day,
Sink, clamorous, like mill-waters, at wild play,
    By turns in every copse:

3

Each tree heart-deep the wrangling rout receives,—
    Save for the whirr within,
You could not tell the starlings from the leaves;
Then one great puff of wings, and the swarm
  heaves
    Away with all its din.

4

Even thus Hope's hours, in ever-eddying flight,
    To many a refuge tend;
With the first light she laughed, and the last
  light
Glows round her still; who natheless in the
  night
    At length must make an end.

5

And now the mustering rooks innumerable
    Together sail and soar,
While for the day's death, like a tolling knell,
Unto the heart they seem to cry, Farewell,
    No more, farewell, no more!

6

Is Hope not plumed, as 'twere a fiery dart?
    And oh! thou dying day,
Even as thou goest must she too depart,
And Sorrow fold such pinions on the heart
    As will not fly away?

Dante Gabriel Rossetti (1828–1882)

The Eagle

He clasps the crag with crooked hands;
Close to the sun in lonely lands,
Ring'd with the azure world, he stands.

The wrinkled sea beneath him crawls;
He watches from his mountain walls,
And like a thunderbolt he falls.

Alfred Lord Tennyson (1809–1892)

To the Man-of-War Bird

Thou who hast slept all night upon the storm,
Waking renew'd on thy prodigious pinions,
(Burst the wild storm? above it thou
   ascended'st,
And rested on the sky, thy slave that cradled
   thee,)
Now a blue point, far, far in heaven floating,
As to the light emerging here on deck I watch
   thee,
(Myself a speck, a point on the world's floating
   vast.)

Far, far at sea,
After the night's fierce drifts have strewn the
   shore with wrecks,
With re-appearing day as now so happy and
   serene,
The rosy and elastic dawn, the flashing sun,
The limpid spread of air cerulean,
Thou also re-appearest.

Thou born to match the gale, (thou art all
    wings,)
To cope with heaven and earth and sea and
    hurricane,
Thou ship of air that never furl'st thy sails,
Days, even weeks untired and onward,
    through spaces, realms gyrating,
At dusk thou look'st on Senegal, at morn
    America,
That sport'st amid the lightning flash and
    thunder-cloud,
In them in thy experiences, had'st thou my
    soul,
What joys! what joys were thine!

Walt Whitman (1819–1892)

The Dalliance of the Eagles

Skirting the river road, (my forenoon walk, my
    rest),
Skyward in air a sudden muffled sound, the
    dalliance of the eagles,
The rushing amorous contact high in space
    together,
The clinching interlocking claws, a living,
    fierce, gyrating wheel,
Four beating wings, two beaks, a swirling
    mass tight grappling,
In tumbling turning clustering loops, straight
    downward falling,
Till o'er the river poised, the twain yet one, a
    moment's lull,
A motionless still balance in the air, then
    parting, talons loosing,
Upward again on slow-firm pinions slanting,
    their separate diverse flight,
She hers, he his, pursuing.

Walt Whitman (1819–1892)

Pain or Joy

Hark! that's the nightingale,
  Telling the selfsame tale
Her song told when this ancient earth was
  young:
So echoes answered when her song was sung
  In the first wooded vale.

We call it love and pain
  The passion of her strain;
And yet we little understand or know;
Why should it not be rather joy that so
  Throbs in each throbbing vein?

Christina Rossetti (1830–1894)

To a Lark

O little singing bird,
  If I could word
In as sweet human phrase
  Thy hymn of praise:

The world should hearken me
  As I do thee,
And I should heed no more
  Than thou, but soar.

Francis William Bourdillon (1852–1921)

Song of a Nest

A song of a nest:—
There was once a nest in a hollow:
Down the mosses and knot-grass pressed,
Soft and warm, and full to the brim—
Vetches leaned over it purple and dim,
With buttercup buds to follow.

I pray you hear my song of a nest,
For it is not long:—
You shall never light, in a summer quest
The bushes among—
Shall never light on a prouder sitter,
A fairer nestful, nor ever know
A softer sound than their tender twitter,
That wind-like did come and go.

Jean Ingelow (1830–1897)

Evolution

Out of the dusk a shadow,
   Then, a spark;
Out of the cloud a silence,
   Then, a lark;
Out of the heart a rapture,
   Then, a pain;
Out of the dead cold ashes,
   Life again.

John Banister Tabb (1845–1909)

A Remonstrance

Sing me no more, sweet warbler, for the dart
Of joy is keener than the flash of pain:
Sing me no more, for the re-echoed strain
Together with the silence breaks my heart.

John Banister Tabb (1845–1909)

TWENTIETH CENTURY

The Blinded Bird

I

So zestfully canst thou sing?
And all this indignity,
With God's consent, on thee!
Blinded ere yet a-wing
By the red-hot needle thou,
I stand and wonder how
So zestfully thou canst sing!

2

Resenting not such wrong,
Thy grievous pain forgot,
Eternal dark thy lot,
Groping thy whole life long,
After that stab of fire;
Enjailed in pitiless wire;
Resenting not such wrong!

3

Who hath charity? This bird.
Who suffereth long and is kind,
Is not provoked, though blind

And alive ensepulchred?
Who hopeth, endureth all things?
Who thinketh no evil, but sings?
Who is divine? This bird.

Thomas Hardy (1840–1928)

The Robin

When up aloft
I fly and fly,
I see in pools
The shining sky,
And a happy bird
Am I, am I!

When I descend
Towards their brink
I stand, and look,
And stoop, and drink,
And bathe my wings,
And chink and prink.

When winter frost
Makes earth as steel,
I search and search
But find no meal,
And most unhappy
Then I feel.

But when it lasts,
And snows still fall,

I get to feel
No grief at all,
For I turn to a cold stiff
Feathery ball!

Thomas Hardy (1840–1928)

The Fifteen Acres

I cling and swing
    On a branch, or sing
Through the cool, clear hush of morning, O:
    Or fling my wing
    In the air, and bring
To sleepier birds a warning, O:
    That the night's in flight,
    And the sun's in sight,
And the dew is the grass adorning, O:
    And the green leaves swing
    As I sing, sing, sing,
    Up by the river,
    Down the dell,
    To the little wee nest,
    Where the big tree fell,
So early in the morning, O.

I flit and twit
    In the sun for a bit
When his light so bright is shining, O:
    Or sit and fit
    My plumes, or knit

Straw plaits for the nest's nice lining, O:
    And she with glee
    Shows unto me
Underneath her wings reclining, O:
    And I sing that Peg
    Has an egg, egg, egg,
    Up by the oat-field,
    Round the mill,
    Past the meadow,
    Down the hill,
So early in the morning, O.

    I stoop and swoop
    On the air, or loop
Through the trees, and then go soaring, O:
    To group with a troop
    On the gusty poop
While the wind behind is roaring, O:
    I skim and swim
    By a cloud's red rim
And up to the azure flooring, O:
    And my wide wings drip
    As I slip, slip, slip
    Down through the rain-drops,
    Back where Peg

Broods in the nest
On the little white egg,
So early in the morning, O.

James Stephens (1880–1950)

To a Linnet in a Cage

When Spring is in the fields that stained your
   wing,
   And the blue distance is alive with song,
And finny quiets of the gabbling spring
   Rock lilies red and long,
At dewy daybreak, I will set you free
   In ferny turnings of the woodbine lane,
Where faint-voiced echoes leave and cross in
   glee
   The hilly swollen plain.

In draughty houses you forget your tune,
   The modulator of the changing hours,
You want the wide air of the moody noon,
   And the slanting evening showers.
So I will loose you, and your song shall fall
   When morn is white upon the dewy pane,
Across my eyelids, and my soul recall
   From worlds of sleeping pain.

Francis Ledwidge (1887–1917)

Magpies in Picardy

The magpies in Picardy
Are more than I can tell.
They flicker down the dusty roads
And cast a magpie spell
On the men who march through Picardy,
Through Picardy to Hell.
(The blackbird flies with panic,
The swallows go like light,
The finches move like ladies,
The owl floats by at night;
But the great and flashing magpie
He flies as artists might.)

A magpie in Picardy
Told me secret things—
Of the music in white feathers
And the sunlight that sings
And dances in deep shadows—
He told me with his wings.
(The hawk is cruel and rigid,
He watches from a height;
The rook is slow and sombre,

The robin loves to fight;
But the great and flashing magpie
He flies as lovers might.)

He told me that in Picardy,
An age ago or more,
While all his feathers still were eggs,
Those dusty highways bore
Brown singing soldiers marching out
Through Picardy to war.
He said that still through chaos
Works on the ancient plan,
And two things have altered not
Since first the world began—
The beauty of the wild green earth
And the bravery of man.
(For the sparrow flies unthinking
And quarrels in his flight;
The heron trails his legs behind,
The lark goes out of sight;
But the great and flashing magpie
He flies as poets might.)

T. P. Cameron Wilson (1888–1918)

Augury

What sweeter sight can ever charm the eye
Than robin come to claim his largess old,
And, pinnacled against the eager sky,
Daring the armies of the brazen cold?
And wren a-running (while the storm
    shrouds all
The swinging mill-sails and black ghosts of
    groves)
Among the weeds that shake beneath the wall,
Well may she vie with him in all our loves!

The mystery of the dark birthday of spring
Ever to childhood flowered into a sign
As over head I saw the paired swans wing,
In whose wild breasts the gods made the light
    shine!
And flight and song have measured year on
    year,
Recorders of my solitude, till the sun
Is the bright hymn of nations of the air
And evening and the dream-like owl are one.

So copses green start out of time stol'n hence
Because they rung with nightingales above
Their fellows, so returns dear innocence
At recollection of the lulling dove;
For alms the redbreast comes, the wren dares
  run,
While rook and magpie saunter through the
  sky,
All with their kinship of the morning sun—
In what rare element they sing and fly!

But O how bitter burns these fair ones' pain,
When satyr hands in cages shut their young,
The old birds coming with their food in vain,
Till death's a mercy; O how vast the wrong
That shuts them in, that starves but one small
  owl
Snatched into glaring day and mocks his hate;
And who, the wonder is, but djinn or ghoul
Durst steal one mothering wing for folly's
  bait?

Edmund Blunden (1896–1974)

In Early Spring

O Spring, I know thee! Seek for sweet surprise
 In the young children's eyes.
But I have learnt the years, and know the yet
 Leaf-folded violet.
Mine ear, awake to silence, can foretell
 The cuckoo's fitful bell.
I wander in a grey time that encloses
 June and the wild hedge-roses.
A year's procession of the flowers doth pass
 My feet, along the grass.
And all you wild birds silent yet, I know
 The notes that stir you so,
Your songs yet half devized in the dim dear
 Beginnings of the year.
In these young days you meditate your part;
 I have it all by heart
I know the secrets of the seeds of flowers
 Hidden and warm with showers,
And how, in kindling Spring, the cuckoo shall
 Alter his interval.
But not a flower or song I ponder is
 My own, but memory's.

I shall be silent in those days desired
    Before a world inspired.
O all brown birds, compose your old song-
  phrases,
    Earth, thy familiar daisies!

A poet mused upon the dusky height,
    Between two stars towards night,
His purpose in his heart. I watched, a space,
    The meaning of his face:
There was the secret, fled from earth and skies,
    Hid in his young grey eyes.
My heart and all the Summer wait his choice,
    And wonder for his voice.
Who shall foretell his songs, and who aspire
    But to divine his lyre?
Sweet earth, we know thy dimmest mysteries,
    But he is lord of his.

Alice Meynell (1847–1922)

The Return of the Goldfinches

We are much honoured by your choice,
O golden birds of silver voice,
That in our garden you should find
A pleasaunce to your mind—

The painted pear of all our trees,
The south slope towards the gooseberries
Where all day long the sun is warm—
Combining use with charm.

Did the pink tulips take your eye?
Or Breach's barn secure and high
To guard you from some chance mishap
Of gales through Shoreham gap?

First you were spied a flighting pair
Flashing and fluting here and there,
Until in stealth the nest was made
And graciously you stayed.

Now when I pause beneath your tree
An anxious head peeps down at me,
A crimson jewel in its crown,
I looking up, you down:—

I wonder if my stripey shawl
Seems pleasant in your eyes at all,
I can assure you that your wings
Are most delightful things.

Sweet birds, I pray, be not severe,
Do not deplore our presence here,
We cannot all be goldfinches
In such a world as this.

The shaded lawn, the bordered flowers,
We'll call them yours instead of ours,
The pinks and the acacia tree
Shall own your sovereignty.

And, if you let us, we will prove
Our lowly and obsequious love,
And when your little grey-pates hatch
We'll help you to keep watch.

No prowling stranger cats shall come
About your high celestial home,
With dangerous sounds we'll chase them hence
And ask no recompense.

And he, the Ethiope of our house,
Slayer of beetle and of mouse,
Huge, lazy, fond, whom we love well—
Peter shall wear a bell.

Believe me, birds, you need not fear,
No cages or limed twigs are here,
We only ask to live with you
In this green garden, too.

And when in other shining summers
Our place is taken by new-comers,
We'll leave them with the house and hill
The goldfinches' good will.

Your dainty flights, your painted coats,
The silver mist that is your notes,
And all your sweet caressing ways
Shall decorate their days.

And never will the thought of spring
Visit our minds, but a gold wing
Will flash among the green and blue,
And we'll remember you.

Sylvia Lynd (1888–1952)

Summer Dusk

Now may we follow on his curving flight,
The white owl mousing in the failing light;
And from the osiers in the river meads,
Hear the sedge-warbler, chiding in the reeds.

Pamela Tennant (1871–1928)

The Gift

You heavens proud above this earth,
  Have you no shade but blue?
Your flow'ring stars are all alike,
  But gold and silver hue:
Your sun but one big iris-flower,
Your clouds are fair but pass in shower;
Live there in your huge sky
The hedge-rose or the campion
  Or purple dragon-fly?

Poor beggar sky! to you we'll send
  Out of our earthly store,
Out of our thousand, thousand sights
  And then a million more,
From all our shapes and colours fine,
From all our unthrift beauty's mine,
  A crumb from all our feast,
A gem from all our treasury,
  The lark—our best and least.

Anon.

Index of Poets

Index of Titles

Index of First Lines